Princess
ANGELICA
Camp Catastrophe

Princess
ANGELICA
Camp Catastrophe

Monique Polak

Illustrated by **Jane Heinrichs**

ORCA BOOK PUBLISHERS

Library and Archives Canada Cataloguing in Publication

Polak, Monique, author
Princess Angelica, camp catastrophe / Monique Polak ; illustrated
by Jane Heinrichs.
(Orca echoes)

Issued in print and electronic formats.
ISBN 978-1-4598-1538-4 (softcover).—ISBN 978-1-4598-1539-1 (PDF).—
ISBN 978-1-4598-1540-7 (EPUB)

I. Heinrichs, Jane, 1982-, illustrator II. Title. III. Series: Orca echoes

PS8631.O43P75 2018   jC813'.6   C2017-904491-5
                           C2017-904492-3

First published in the United States, 2018
Library of Congress Control Number: 2017949724

Summary: In this early chapter book, Angelica is mistaken for a princess
on her way to summer camp.

Orca Book Publishers gratefully acknowledges the support for its publishing programs
provided by the following agencies: the Government of Canada through the Canada Book Fund
and the Canada Council for the Arts, and the Province of British Columbia
through the BC Arts Council and the Book Publishing Tax Credit.

Edited by Liz Kemp
Cover artwork and interior illustrations by Jane Heinrichs
Author photo by Terence Byrnes

ORCA BOOK PUBLISHERS
www.orcabook.com

Printed and bound in Canada.

21 20 19 18 • 4 3 2 1

For the real-life Angelica,
Angelica Antonakopoulos, aka Jelly,
who helped inspire this story.
—MP

In memory of my dad, who took me
on wonderful canoe trips down the
Red River and fishing in the Whiteshell.
—JH

Chapter One

"Did I ever tell you we have an elevator?" I ask Maddie.

Her brown eyes widen. "You never mentioned it. But that is seriously cool. Where is it?"

Maddie believes all my stories. It's one of the reasons she's my best friend.

Another reason is that she is super kind. It also helps that Maddie lives two doors down, which is handy, especially during snowstorms.

"Our elevator is at the back of my parents' closet."

"Where does it go to?"

Maddie always asks a lot of questions. Luckily, I am great at coming up with answers.

"To the attic."

"Can we ride it?"

I was hoping she would ask. "Yup. There's just one hitch." I pause. That will make her even more eager for a ride on our elevator. "I have to blindfold you." I make it sound like blindfolding your best friend is no big deal.

"Blindfold me? Jelly, is this one of your stories?"

I make a huffing sound so she will know I am insulted. "Of *course* not.

The blindfold is for insurance purposes. So you won't sue." My parents are both lawyers, so I know a lot about suing.

When we get to my parents' bedroom, I grab a dark scarf from my mother's drawer and tie it over Maddie's eyes.

"Can you see anything?"

"Not a thing."

"Perfect."

I spin her around three times. Then I lead her into my parents' closet. I guide her so she doesn't trip over the shoes and boots. "Okay," I tell her. "We're inside the elevator now."

I clang together two wire hangers and stamp my feet on the closet floor. "Whoa," I say. "We're going up. I feel it in my stomach."

"Me too," says Maddie.

I grin. My plan is working.

"What's up in your attic?" she asks.

"Skeletons." It's the first thing that pops into my head.

"Cool."

"We're nearly there," I tell her. I clang together the wire hangers again. "The elevator doors are about to open."

"I can't believe I have a friend who has her own elevator," Maddie says to herself.

"We're there." I grab her elbow and lead her out of the closet. "Are you ready to see skeletons? Do you promise you won't sue?"

"Yes and yes." Maddie's voice catches in her throat. That is probably because she has never seen a skeleton before.

I spin Maddie around three more times—and untie the scarf. "Ta-dum!"

Maddie is trembling.

Because the lights are out in my parents' bedroom, it takes her a minute to realize what's going on.

There are no skeletons.

We are not in the attic.

There is no elevator.

Maddie hops up and down. "Jelly," she cries out, "you made that story up!"

There is another reason why Maddie is my best friend.

Other kids might get angry.

Not Maddie.

Because a second later, the two of us are laughing so hard we end up rolling around on the floor in my parents' bedroom.

Chapter Two

The yellow school bus is waiting in the parking lot. The driver supervises as parents stow their kids' duffel bags in the bottom hatch. Counselors are wandering around, checking in with parents and campers.

I take a deep breath. I've slept over at Maddie's house plenty of times, but this is my first time going to sleepaway camp, and Maddie is not coming. Her *grandmaman* from France is visiting this summer.

Mom hugs me tight. "We'll miss you, Angelica." Then she whispers into my hair, "It might be wise to keep your storytelling under control while you are with new friends."

Dad hugs me next. "We love you, Jelly."

I watch as they walk back to the car. Before Dad gets in, he turns to give me one last wave. "Have a great adventure, Princess! The royal court won't be the same without you!" he calls out.

Mom shakes her head. She doesn't like Dad calling me Princess. She thinks it encourages gender stereotypes and snobbishness.

A girl with red hair and freckles is waiting to get on the bus too. She looks at me, then at her sandals, then back at me. "Your dad still calls you Princess?"

she says. "That's silly. Unless, of course, you really are one."

An idea begins to form in my head. I throw back my shoulders and straighten my posture. I can practically feel the crown on my head. "As a matter of fact, I *am* a princess. Princess Angelica." Instead of offering her my hand for shaking, I give her a regal nod.

"Jenna Trudel," she says a little nervously. Then she curtsies, something that is not that easy to do when you are standing in a line. "I didn't know princesses went to camp."

"We don't usually. My parents thought it would be good for me to get a break from the royal court. All that fine food."

Jenna has trouble looking me in the eye. She is obviously not used to making small talk with royalty. "Your parents," she says. "The king and queen. I think I saw them in the parking lot."

I consider what Jenna might have seen—my mom snapping a photo of me on her phone, my dad in his khakis. "Those weren't my parents," I tell her. "They were my lady- and gentleman-in-waiting. Hey, do you want to sit together on the bus?"

Jenna grins. "It would be an honor," she says, and then she adds, "Your Majesty."

There are hardly any seats left on the bus. Kids are telling jokes, and the girls in the seat behind us are singing "The Wheels on the Bus." The counselors are walking up and down the aisles, taking attendance.

"Where'd the bus driver go?" a boy's voice calls from the back seat. "If we don't hurry, we'll miss afternoon swim!"

The air smells like sunscreen, tuna sandwiches and stale vomit. I reach over and slide the window open. I spot the bus driver outside. He is wiping his forehead and looking distressed. "What's wrong with you?" I hear him ask.

At first I think he's talking to some kid who refuses to get on the bus, but when he says, "You always close. I don't know why you won't close today," I realize he is addressing the luggage hatch underneath the bus. More precisely, the door to the luggage hatch.

I lean out the window and watch as he slams it shut. The hatch pops back open. Even when the driver kicks it, it still does not stay shut.

"Excuse me," I say. "You might try this…" I take a bobby pin out of my hair and hand it to him.

The driver sighs. "What use is a hairpin? This door needs to be replaced. I'd better call the parts department." He checks his watch. "We'll be lucky if we get to camp in time for dinner."

"Before you make that call," I tell the driver, "why don't you at least try wedging in my bobby pin?"

The driver shrugs. "Ridiculous!" he says. But then, probably because he has nothing to lose, he wedges in the bobby pin like I suggested and slams the door shut.

The driver keeps his eyes on the hatch. He is waiting for it to pop open.

But it stays closed.

He rattles the handle, testing my solution. "Who knew?!" The driver gives me a thumbs-up.

When he takes his seat behind the wheel, the kids on the bus break into a chorus of cheers.

Jenna looks really impressed. "How did you know that would fix the door?"

"I just thought it might. What's the big deal?" I ask her.

"Well...I just never thought...you know...I guess I thought princesses just sat on their thrones and looked pretty and got spoiled."

"FYI," I tell her, "Princess Angelica is not the sitting-around type."

Chapter Three

Our cabin is called Pinecone. Jenna and I share it with two other girls, Joon and Amber. Our counselor, Terry-Anne, is responsible for two bunks—Pinecone and Maple Leaf, which is just across the gravel path.

Terry-Anne is over at Maple Leaf. She must be explaining to the girls there the things she just explained to us—the linens for our cots are in the closet, and we have to make our own beds every morning and keep the cabin tidy.

Terry-Anne also explained that the cabins don't have their own bathrooms. We share an outhouse with the girls from Maple Leaf.

The outhouse is not as bad as it sounds. It is small, but it smells like the woods, and there is plenty of toilet paper. When I get back from using it, I know from Joon's and Amber's sideway glances that Jenna has told them I am royalty.

My hunch is confirmed when Joon offers to make up my cot. And also when I complain that my pillow is too hard and Amber offers to trade and give me hers, which is softer.

"I like the corners tucked in," I tell Joon as she pulls my blanket over the sheets.

"You're right, this is softer," I tell Amber when I test her pillow.

After the beds are made, we unpack our bags. We all share one dresser. The girls insist I take the top drawer, which is the largest.

"Do we call you Princess Angelica? Or do you prefer Your Majesty?" Joon asks when we have finished unpacking and are lying on our cots.

"Either one is fine," I tell her.

"Well then, Princess Angelica, do you mind telling us about the royal court?" Amber asks.

Now is the perfect moment to tell the truth, to confess that I am not really a princess. But I don't want my new friends to think I'm a liar. Besides, if they knew I was just a regular girl like them, they wouldn't look at me the way they are looking at me now. They wouldn't think I was special, and they wouldn't be so eager to hear my stories. I adjust myself on the bed. "Certainly." I close my eyes. My imagination works best when my eyes are shut.

"I come from a kingdom very far away," I begin.

"Is it in Europe?" Jenna asks. "Or Asia?"

"My parents are from Asia," Joon says.

"I'm afraid I can't divulge the precise location. For security reasons. But I can tell you that I live in a humongous stone castle surrounded by a moat filled with crocodiles."

"Crocodiles? Isn't that dangerous?" Joon asks.

"No, they only eat intruders. The crocodiles have known me since I was

a baby. They let me ride on their backs. They're better than floaties—or rafts."

"What's your room like?" Amber asks.

"My room is at the top of a turret. I have my own elevator."

"I bet there isn't an outhouse," Jenna says.

"Of course not. I have an en suite bathroom. With a Jacuzzi, which is constantly filled with jelly-bean-scented bubble bath."

"Wow," Joon says. "I love jelly beans. What's the furniture like in your royal bedroom?"

"It's all gold. Even the canopy over my bed is gold. Eighteen carat."

I open my eyes. My cot is by the window. Outside, the sky is turning gray. A gust of wind makes the checkered curtains rustle. "The curtains in my royal bedroom are purple velvet, and they go *swish*. I find the sound very relaxing. Did I mention the round-the-clock room service? If I want a milkshake— or a chocolate éclair—I text the royal kitchen and presto! Someone brings it right up. The milkshake comes in a silver goblet."

I can hear Joon licking her lips. "Chocolate éclairs are my favorite dessert in all the world," she says.

My eyes land on the night table between my cot and Jenna's. There is a book called *Scariest Stories Ever* on Jenna's side of the table. "There's a wonderful library in the castle. All I have to do is *think* about the sort of book I'd like to read. Next thing I know, it comes sliding down a golden chute and lands at the foot of my bed."

Amber sits up in her cot. "I don't understand. If all you have to do is *think* of a book…why doesn't it work that way with the food too? You said if you get hungry, you text the royal kitchen. Why couldn't you just *think* of a milkshake, and they would send it through the golden chute?"

Luckily, coming up with quick answers is one of my talents. "Because it would spill," I tell her.

Jenna nods. "Of course it would."

"I guess." Amber does not sound convinced. I hope she won't ask for her pillow back.

"What kinds of things do you do at the royal court?" Joon asks. "Besides eating and reading and taking bubble baths and swimming with your crocodiles?"

"I fix things."

Amber rolls over on her cot and opens her eyes so she is looking right at me. "You fix things? That doesn't sound very princess-y. Aren't there staff around to fix things for you?"

"Of course there are. But I happen to enjoy fixing things."

"Princess Angelica fixed the luggage hatch on the bus," Jenna chimes in.

Outside, it has begun to rain. I guess there will be no free swim this afternoon.

A plump raindrop lands on Amber's forehead. It is followed by another, plumper raindrop.

There is a leak in the roof right over Amber's cot.

"I'll get the tin pail from the porch," Joon offers.

Amber puts the pail under the leaky spot. Every droplet makes a *ping* when it lands inside the pail. "You don't actually think I'm going to be able to sleep with

this pail next to me and all that *pinging*, do you?" Amber asks.

She turns to me. "If you enjoy fixing things, Princess Angelica, why don't you do something about our roof?"

Chapter Four

Lining the tin pail with a towel was my idea. The roof kept leaking, but at least the *pinging* stopped.

In the morning the sun is shining. The only memory of last night's rain is the bucket, which Amber empties into the flower box on the porch.

I tell the other girls in my bunk it's better not to tell Terry-Anne I am royalty.

"I don't want any extra-special treatment," I explain.

Amber gives me a sidelong look. "If it were me," she says, "I'd want all the extra-special treatment I could get."

"I've had extra-special treatment all my life. I'm curious to know what life is like as a *commoner*."

When Terry-Ann hears about the leaky roof, she texts the camp director. The director texts back to say that Leonard, the handyman, is repairing the dock. The roof will have to wait until tomorrow or even the day after. "They're forecasting more rain tonight. I'm afraid you'll need to use the bucket again," Terry-Anne tells Amber.

Terry-Anne turns to me. "Lining the bucket was a great idea, Angelica." The compliment makes me glow.

The other girls are discussing what to wear to breakfast.

"Can you believe there's no full-length mirror in this cabin?" Amber says.

"Do these shorts look okay?" Jenna wants to know.

Amber forgot to pack her hair goop. "Can I borrow some of yours?" she asks me.

"I don't use any. I also don't worry about how my shorts look. And I don't have a full-length mirror."

Joon gasps. "You live in a castle and you don't have a full-length mirror?"

Jenna comes up with an explanation for me. "I bet Princess Angelica's lady-in-waiting chooses her outfits and tells her whether to tuck her shirt in or out. Am I right, Your Highness?"

"I do have a lady-in-waiting, and a gentleman-in-waiting too. They're the ones who took me to the bus. But in our kingdom, we don't fuss about what to wear or how we look. Kids have more important things on their minds—what we like to call *higher pursuits*."

"Speaking of high," Amber says, "Your *High*ness, I spotted a ladder by the outhouse. Didn't you say you'd have a look at the roof?"

Jenna crosses her arms over her chest. "Princess Angelica never said anything abou—"

I stretch out my arm. It's my royal signal to let Jenna know I can deal with Amber. "I'll look at the roof now."

I make sure the ladder's feet are firmly planted on the ground. When I climb past the window of our bunk, I see that Jenna is modeling another pair of shorts and Amber is braiding Joon's hair.

When I get to the third-to-last rung of the ladder, I can see the roof. It's flat and covered with tar. I know I shouldn't step onto it. If something goes wrong, the camp could get sued. But I want to show off my repair skills to Amber and the others. It's a good thing I positioned the ladder close to the section of roof over Amber's bed. Because when I lean over to inspect the roof's surface, I spot a crack in the roof and a small hole, just a bit bigger than a quarter.

Ah-ha.

A hairpin won't help. Duct tape would come loose in the rain.

I close my eyes. Coming up with solutions requires as much imagination as inventing stories.

Maybe my nose works better because my eyes are closed. Or maybe last night's rain is making the smells around me stronger. For a moment my nostrils are filled with the clean, sharp scent of pine. I take a deep, delicious sniff.

That's when I remember something we learned in science class. Tar can be made from the sap of a pine tree.

I smile as I open my eyes. In every direction I look, I see trees. Hundreds of pine trees.

It's also a good thing that it's hot outside. Sap will be oozing from the pines.

After breakfast I find an empty tuna can in the recycling. The can is perfect for collecting sap. After lunch Jenna and I borrow a knife from the camp kitchen. On our way out I spot a length of old cord. "We'll need that too," I tell Jenna.

Once we are in the pines, we choose a large, healthy-looking tree. I use the knife to pry away a section of bark, then carve out a V shape. "Hand me the can," I tell Jenna, "and the cord." Jenna helps me tie the can into position under the V. "Bingo!" I say when the first drop of sap lands in the can.

"Have you heard the expression *A watched pot never boils?*" I ask Jenna. "It's the same for collecting sap. A watched tuna can never fills up. We should do something else while we wait for the sap to collect." It's Jenna's idea to lie in the grass and watch the clouds.

Later, when we check on the can, there seems to be enough sap to make tar. After all, the hole in the roof isn't very big. On the way back to Pinecone, we pass the girls from Maple Leaf. They're making a midmorning treat of s'mores at the fire pit, but Jenna and I are too busy to stop and join in. "Will you smear the sap over the hole?" she asks.

"First I need to mix in some wax."

"How do you know stuff like that?"

"We learned it in science," I tell her. Then I add, "At the royal court."

There are candles in our bunk—in case the electricity goes out. I break off a chunk of candle and add it to the sap.

Jenna and I head back to the fire pit where the campers from Maple Leaf are. "Stand back," I tell Jenna when I place the can on the warm rocks beside the fire.

I use a twig to stir it.

"What exactly are you girls up to?" Terry-Anne has come to check on us.

"I'm showing Jenna how to make tar," I tell her. "It's a science experiment."

"I'm all for science experiments," Terry-Anne says. "Just don't get hurt."

"Of course not," Jenna tells her. "We promise to be careful."

After the mixture has cooled, I ask Jenna if she wants to come up the ladder with me.

"Uh, I don't think so," she says. "How about I hold it? To protect Your Royal Highness."

"That's very considerate."

I climb back up and use the twig to apply the tar.

"How did it go?" Jenna asks as I'm coming down the ladder.

"Perfectly," I say regally.

Chapter Five

"Jelly?" I hear someone call out in the dining hall.

"Yes?" I raise my hand in the air and look around to see who wants me.

Every cabin has its own table. Ours is table six. Jenna sits next to me. Amber and Joon are across from us.

"*Jelly*?" Amber is laughing. "Is that your nickname? If you ask me, it's a terrible nickname for a princess. It doesn't sound very *royal*."

"Jelly?"

The person calling out *jelly* is wearing a white apron and a hairnet. He must work in the camp kitchen. He is holding up a jumbo-size jar of red jelly. "Anybody here want jelly on their sandwich?" he asks.

"I do!" I say. And though I prefer a plain cream-cheese sandwich, I spread a thick layer of jelly on one half of my bagel. "Nickname?" I say to Amber after I have taken a bite and wiped the jelly from the side of my mouth. "What are you talking about?"

After lunch there is swimming, then kayaking and arts and crafts. Before dinner Terry-Anne sits us down to tell us all about our upcoming overnight kayaking trip. We'll be paddling twenty miles in total and sleeping overnight in tents.

After dinner, we sing by the campfire and roast marshmallows.

Jenna insists on roasting my marshmallows for me. "This one's nice and toasty," she says, handing me a stick with a perfectly roasted marshmallow dangling off it.

"Thank you. It's delicious."

"It's really an honor to make you a marshmallow."

The rain starts up again almost as soon as we are in our pajamas. "You'd better hand me the bucket," Amber tells Joon.

"You won't be needing the bucket anymore," Jenna tells Amber and Joon. "Princess Angelica fixed the leak. She used pine sap mixed with candle wax."

"I'll take the bucket," Amber says, shooting me a look. "Just in case."

I get the feeling Amber is disappointed when, even after the rain picks up, there isn't a single drip.

Nine o'clock is lights-out.

Joon turns on her flashlight. She is sitting up on her elbows. "Wanna pull an all-nighter?" she asks.

Jenna has rolled over to face the wall, but now she turns around. "What's an all-nighter?"

"It's when you stay up all night telling stories," Joon explains.

Jenna yawns. "What if we're too tired for activities tomorrow?"

Joon sighs. "It's not summer camp if we don't pull at least one all-nighter. Besides, don't you want to hear more stories about Princess Angelica's life at the royal court?"

I can feel my eyelids getting heavy, but the other girls keep me awake with questions.

"Do you go to school at the royal court?" Joon asks.

"I have private tutors for every subject. They are renowned experts in their fields. My English teacher is a published poet. My gym teacher won a gold medal in the Olympics for pole vaulting. My art teacher is the curator of our national museum."

Amber drums on the bucket. "Who taught you how to do repairs?" she asks. "Was it the pole-vaulting champion?"

"Of course not. I learned from my... my lady-in-waiting. She's very handy."

"What about your parents, the king and queen? You don't mention them very much. What are they like?" Jenna asks.

"Oh, they're wonderful, of course. But they're busy running the kingdom and attending parties."

"Have you met the Duchess of Cambridge?" Jenna wants to know.

"You mean my auntie Kate? She comes to all my birthday parties."

"Wow," Jenna says.

Amber clears her throat. "If you don't mind my asking, Princess Angelica, what exactly does a princess do?"

"You mean besides lessons and repairs to the castle?" I wonder if Amber knows I am stalling.

"I mean…what's the point in being a princess?" Amber asks.

Once again Jenna answers for me. "In the modern world," she says, "royals act like ambassadors. They forge relationships between countries. Princesses have the power to influence other important people. As a princess, Angelica can use her power to help fix our world. It sure needs fixing."

"Why, thank you, Jenna," I say. "I couldn't have expressed it better. I will do my utmost to live up to that job description."

"Glad to be of service, Your Majesty."

Chapter Six

I really like being a princess.

I like how Jenna roasts all of my marshmallows and Joon insists on making up my cot in the morning. I especially like inventing stories about the royal court.

I catch myself standing taller than usual and throwing back my shoulders when I speak. I think it's because I am starting to *feel* like a princess.

There's only one small problem. Visiting day.

It's coming up next Sunday. I am afraid my parents will blow my cover.

So I try writing them a letter.

Dear Mom and Dad,

Jenna peers over my shoulder. "Oh, that's so exciting," she says. "You're writing to a king and queen."

I cover the sheet with my hand. "If you don't mind."

Jenna bites her lip. "Sorry."

Camp is awesome. I get along with all the girls in my cabin. Our roof was leaking and guess who FIXED IT? Mom, I know you warned me not to get carried away with my storytelling, but, well...things have gotten kind of out of hand.

So if you don't mind, when you come on visiting day, could you tell my friends that you and Dad are my lady- and gentleman-in-waiting?

With love, Princess Angelica (aka Jelly)

I read over what I have written. Then I tear up the paper into small pieces so no one will be able to put it back together.

Who am I kidding? My mom and dad will never go along with that scheme.

There is only one solution.

I am going to have to tell the truth.

"Is something wrong?" Jenna asks. "Do you have writer's block?"

"No," I say to Jenna. "It's just that... well...to be honest..."

I am about to tell Jenna I am not really a royal when the door to our cabin flies open.

It's Joon, and she has something feathery in her hands. At first I think it's

a purple bird, but then I realize it's a pen. A purple feather pen.

"I just got this in my care package," she says. "It's for you, Princess Angelica. My parents sent it. I guess they got excited when I wrote to tell them I was bunking with royalty. Do you like it?"

"Of course I like it," I say, taking the pen from Joon and testing it on a fresh sheet of paper. "It's magnificent. I'll write to thank them, of course."

"Oh," Joon says, "they'll be so excited to get a letter from a princess."

I nod regally and begin my letter to Joon's parents. It is easier to write to them than to write to my parents.

As for telling the other girls the truth, well, that will have to wait for a better time. After all, the girls will be crushed. I don't want to disappoint them, do I?

The letter to Joon's parents practically writes itself. After I have checked my spelling, I draw a royal seal at the bottom of the page. Joon and Jenna watch me. "Usually, the seal would be embossed, which means raised," I tell them. "But the royal embossing machine was too heavy to pack."

"It's a beautiful seal," Jenna says. "Do you think you could write a letter to my parents too?"

Someone knocks at our cabin door. It's Leonard, the handyman. He brings in a folding cot and sets it up in the corner.

"Is another girl moving in?" Jenna asks him.

"Don't ask me," Leonard answers. "I just follow the director's instructions."

Terry-Anne turns up next. "There's a new camper coming to Pinecone," she tells us. "I hope you'll make her feel welcome." Terry-Anne turns to me and gives me a huge smile. "Angelica, you're going to be thrilled when you see who it is."

Terry-Anne pops her head out the cabin door. "Okay," we hear her say, "you can come in now."

The new girl is Maddie.

Under any other circumstances, I would be thrilled.

"Jelly!" Maddie throws her arms around me. "Grandmaman had a change of plans, so my parents signed me up for camp!"

"Jelly?" Amber says. "Did she just call you *Jelly*?"

Amber marches up to Maddie and taps her shoulder. "I take it," she says, "you know Princess Angelica."

I squeeze Maddie's hand and give her a look. I hope this will send the message that I need her to play along.

Maddie does not get the message.

"What? Princess Angelica?" she says. "Princess Angelica?" she says again.

Then Maddie shakes her head and turns to look at me. "Let me guess, Jelly. You've been inventing stories again!"

Chapter Seven

There are two double kayaks and one single kayak. Because there are five of us, and Maddie is new, I figure she will use the single kayak. But that's not what happens.

Amber and Joon claim the yellow double kayak.

Jenna turns to Maddie. "Do you want to share the red one?" she asks her.

"What about me?" I ask, but Jenna ignores me.

That leaves me with the single kayak.

"Look how fast the clouds are moving with the wind," I say to Amber and Joon when I paddle up to them.

Amber and Joon exchange a look but do not say a word. That's when I confirm that Amber, Joon and Jenna are not talking to me.

Maddie waves from the bow of the red kayak. I decide to ignore her. This is all her fault! If she had just gone along with my story, none of this would have happened!

Terry-Anne is in a single kayak too. She paddles at the back of our pack so she can keep an eye on us.

Up ahead, a loon swoops down on the water. "D'you see the loon?" I call out to the others. Terry-Anne is the only one who says she saw it.

I try not to think about the fact that my friends are angry with me. Instead, I make myself concentrate on the cloudy sky and the soothing sound my paddle makes as I dip it in and out of the water.

"You doing okay on your own?" Terry-Anne has paddled her kayak up to mine.

"I'd rather be by myself," I tell her. I wonder if she knows I am lying?

"Amber told me what happened—that you invented some story about being a princess," Terry-Anne says.

I can feel my ears get hot under my sun hat. "I like making up stories." It's all I can think of saying.

"There's nothing wrong with telling stories," Terry-Anne says. "But it isn't right to deceive your friends."

My ears get even hotter. "When do you think they'll start talking to me again?"

Terry-Anne rests her paddle and lets her kayak drift. "Hard to say. Apologizing would probably be a wise first move."

The two of us drift together in silence. In my head, I practice apologizing to my friends. *I'm sorry for deceiving you. But I get a little carried away when I'm inventing stories.*

I suddenly remember something my dad once told me. *It's inadvisable*, he said, *to use the word* but *in an apology. It's better to own up to your mistake. To take responsibility for whatever you've done wrong.*

So when we drag our kayaks up onto the rocky beach where we are stopping for lunch, I decide to get this apologizing business over with.

"I'm sorry for deceiving you," I say to Jenna, Joon and Amber. "Also, I'm not angry with you anymore," I tell Maddie.

Amber crosses her arms over her chest. "You don't sound very sorry."

"I am. Very sorry." I stop myself from adding the *but* part.

Terry-Anne is laying out a checkered cloth on the rocks, but I know she is listening. "It's considered good manners to accept an apology," she tells Amber.

"Fine then! We accept it—*Jelly*."

Something tells me they have not completely forgiven me, but at least they are talking to me again.

I help Terry-Anne unpack the sandwiches from one of the dry bags. There are five cheese and tomato and one with egg salad. The chef must have run out of tomatoes.

"Who wants the egg salad sandwich?" Terry-Anne asks.

"Not me!" Joon says. "That sandwich smells like farts."

When no one else offers to take the smelly sandwich, I say I will. I hope the others will appreciate my gesture.

Over lunch, Terry-Anne explains that we need to paddle five more miles this afternoon to reach our destination, a place called Trout Island. We will have to paddle hard, since the wind is picking up and we want to get there before dark.

I wonder if one of the other girls will offer to take the single kayak and let me ride in a double, but no one does. That's how I know for sure that I haven't been completely forgiven for pretending to be a princess.

Back in our kayaks, Amber and Joon lead the way, and Jenna and Maddie follow close behind. I feel a little lonely when I hear Amber and Joon singing and Jenna and Maddie telling jokes.

I have to paddle extra hard to keep up with them.

"Look out for rocks!" Terry-Anne calls from behind me.

We've reached a part of the lake where the water is shallow and there are giant rock formations sticking out of it.

Maybe it's because Amber and Joon are singing so loudly that they don't hear Terry-Anne's warning.

A *crack!* echoes in the air as the stern of the yellow kayak hits rock.

"What was that?" Amber shouts from the bow.

"We just hit a rock! A big one!" Joon shouts back. "I can't steer!" Joon sounds like she is about to cry.

Terry-Anne paddles past me toward the yellow kayak. "Oh no," I hear her say to herself as she rushes by.

Chapter Eight

The rudder on the yellow kayak is broken. It has snapped off the brace that holds it to the kayak and now dangles loosely from the cables.

"What do we do now?" Amber asks.

"Above all, don't panic," Terry-Anne says. She uses her whistle to alert Jenna and Maddie, who have paddled up ahead, and signals for them to turn back.

Without the rudder, Amber and Joon have trouble keeping their kayak from wobbling. They are still able to paddle, but the yellow kayak keeps shifting around, wanting to move with the wind.

Terry-Anne lines up her kayak next to Amber and Joon's. I paddle to the other side. Amber grabs on to the edge of Terry-Anne's kayak. Joon grabs on to mine. This way, at least, we can give the girls a rest— and keep their kayak moving straight.

"Like I told you, the first thing you need to do is stay calm," Terry-Anne says. "It's possible to kayak without a rudder, but you two aren't used to it, and it takes a lot more effort. But we have to get this kayak back to the beach so I can assess the damage. I'll need to phone the camp director and let her know what's happened."

The wind is against us, so it takes Amber and Joon nearly an hour to get the yellow kayak to shore. Terry-Anne and I stay nearby, encouraging the girls and giving them breaks by holding on to the kayak. Jenna and Maddie paddle in behind us.

"What about Trout Island?" Jenna asks when we are at the beach and Terry-Anne is rummaging through her dry bag for her cell phone.

"Trout Island will still be there next summer," Terry-Anne says. "Even if someone delivered a new kayak this afternoon, there wouldn't be time for us to paddle all the way there."

Terry-Anne's cell phone is inside another small dry bag. When she presses the phone to her ear, she shakes her head. Then she peers at the screen, looking for service bars. "That's strange," she says. "I'm not getting a signal. There's usually service out here."

Joon rubs her belly. "What if we run out of food?"

"We have plenty of food," Terry-Anne assures Joon. "Right now, what we need more than food is a kayak repairman."

I tap Terry-Anne's shoulder. "Did you just say repair*man*? Because I happen to know a good repair*person*."

"Princ—" Jenna stops herself. "I mean, Jelly repaired the luggage hatch on the bus."

"And the leaky roof," Joon adds.

Terry-Anne examines the rudder. "I'm afraid this is going to be a bigger job."

Amber puts her hands on her hips and looks me in the eye. "Can you do it, Jelly?"

I feel five pairs of eyes on me. I want to say yes, but I don't want to make a promise I can't keep. "I'm going to need to study the problem first," I tell the others.

Terry-Anne claps her hands. "All right then," she says, "let's give Jelly some time to study the problem. The rest of you can help me set up the tents. We're camping here tonight."

"But this beach is full of rocks," Joon says.

"It sure is. But it's not as if we have a choice in the matter." Terry-Anne lifts her chin toward the densely forested area beyond the beach. "There's no place for tents back there."

Joon unfolds the groundsheets. Jenna snaps together the tent poles.

I try not to pay attention to the others. Instead, I go over to the yellow

kayak and examine the rudder the way Terry-Anne did when we got to shore. If we had rope I might be able to tie the rudder back into place on the kayak. Only we didn't bring any rope.

Maddie taps my shoulder. "Did you come up with a solution yet?"

"Not yet."

"Do you think you'll come up with one soon?" she asks.

"I don't know. That is not how solutions work. You can't rush them."

Terry-Anne is helping Joon lay out the groundsheets. "Don't bother Jelly," Terry-Anne tells Maddie. "She needs to think. Why don't you help Jenna with the tent poles?"

Examining the rudder is not helping. And it doesn't help to think about how uncomfortable it is going to be to sleep on this rocky beach.

"Oops," I hear someone say. When I look up, I see that Maddie has tripped.

She kicks at the rocky ground. "Dumb bark," she mutters. She reaches down between the rocks to pick up the strip of bark she tripped on.

"Did you just say *dumb bark*?" I ask her.

"I tripped over this thing. I suppose I wasn't paying attention," Maddie says.

Amber is watching us. "It's just a piece of bark, Angelica. Who cares?"

"*I* care," I tell her. "Because thanks to Maddie, I think I just came up with a way to repair the rudder."

"Really?" Maddie takes a bow and laughs.

I point to the forest. There is plenty of bark back there. "We can make rope from bark. Then we can tie the rudder back onto the kayak."

Terry-Anne likes my idea. She tells us that when she took a wilderness survival course, she learned how to make lashing from bark. "Actually," she says, taking the strip of bark from Maddie and turning it over, "it's this fiber behind the bark that makes the best lashing. But before you start peeling bark—" Terry-Anne stops herself and raises one finger in the air. "One request, girls. I only want you taking bark from branches that are lying on the ground or from trees that are dead. Bark is like skin. It protects a tree from disease and insects, and helps it retain moisture and nutrients. Removing it from a live tree can damage it."

Jenna and I look at each other. I know it's because we are both remembering how I stripped the bark off the pine tree so we could collect sap.

"That was an emergency," I tell Jenna.

"This is an even bigger emergency," she says.

Chapter Nine

The longest strips of bark will make the best lashing. Maddie finds a long, thick poplar branch on the ground. When she tries peeling the bark off with her fingers, Terry-Anne stops her. "We'll get longer strips if we use a knife," she says, demonstrating with her camping knife.

Soon we are all hunting for fallen branches or dead trees. Terry-Anne doesn't want us to hurt ourselves, so we bring our pieces to her, and she does the cutting.

Once we have a big enough pile of fiber, we go and sit by the yellow kayak, and Terry-Anne shows us how to make lashing. First she pours a little water over the fibers. "You need to keep this stuff wet. If the fiber starts to dry, it will be too hard to work with," she explains. Terry-Anne picks out a long strip of fiber, folding it in two. One side is longer than the other. As she pinches and twists the fiber, it starts to knot up. Soon we are all making lashing.

The next step is to braid the lashing together so that it will be extra strong. Amber asks to do the braiding. "It's exactly like braiding hair," she says while she works.

It doesn't take her much time to braid a nice long, strong strip. Terry-Anne tugs on each end to test it. We all clap when she nods her approval.

The others watch as I secure the rudder to the kayak, wrapping the braid around the rudder and the metal brace designed to hold it in place.

I leave enough lashing to tie a knot at the bottom.

"I don't get it," Amber says. "Now the rudder won't be able to move at all, which means we won't be able to steer. What good is that?"

"That's true," I say. "The rudder won't be able to move. But that's my plan!" I show Amber and the others how I've attached the rudder to the exact middle of the stern. Then I pull on the rudder, and it doesn't budge. "If the rudder stays in exactly this position, the kayak should move in a straight line."

"I think Jelly's plan is going to work," Terry-Anne adds. "If the rudder is in position, it will help Amber and Joon to be more stable in the water and to move more quickly. Remember how hard it was paddling in a straight line without the rudder? Tomorrow morning, we should all be able to paddle straight back to camp."

"So we won't starve to death after all!" Joon sounds relieved.

"Speaking of starving to death," Terry-Anne says, "how do you girls feel about veggie burgers for dinner?"

"My favorite!" Joon says.

"What food isn't your favorite?" Amber asks her.

After we have unpacked our gear and arranged our sleeping bags in the tents, we gather farther down the beach around a fire pit. Terry-Anne is grilling burgers.

"Those kaiser rolls look delicious," Joon says.

The sky is turning from bluish-purple to black. The air smells of firewood and lake water and roasted garlic.

"Can you please pass the mustard?" Joon asks when Terry-Anne hands the burgers around.

"I know I packed a squeeze jar of mustard," Terry-Anne says, "but I'm afraid it's still in one of the dry bags."

"Is it Dijon?" Joon asks. "Dijon is my absolute favorite mustard."

Terry-Anne is sampling one of her burgers. "I think so," she says, between bites.

Joon pops up from her spot. "I'll get it."

"Watch your step. Why don't you take my flashli—" Terry-Anne begins, but Joon is already running down the beach toward the tents.

The burgers are scrumptious. Terry-Anne is asking whether any of us want seconds when she realizes that Joon has not come back with the mustard.

"Joon?" Terry-Anne calls into the darkness. "Did you find the mustard?"

When there is no answer, Terry-Anne stands up and calls again.

Still no answer.

When Terry-Anne turns on her flashlight, I notice she is chewing her lip. "I'm going to look for her," she says.

Amber offers to come along.

"Okay," Terry-Anne says. "The rest of you stay here by the campfire. We'll roast marshmallows once Joon's back."

Maddie comes up with the idea of telling stories. "That's what you're supposed to do 'round a campfire, right?" she says.

Jenna nudges me. "You start, Jelly!"

For once, my heart isn't into telling stories. "What do you think is taking them so long?" I ask.

That's when we hear footsteps on the rocks—and Terry-Anne's voice. "Let's bring her this way," Terry-Anne is saying. Her flashlight casts an eerie pool of white light. Terry-Anne and Amber have found Joon, but she is slumped over, propped up between them like a bag of potatoes.

"Is she dead?" Jenna asks.

"Of course I'm not dead." Joon's voice sounds shaky.

"We found her on the ground. She must've tripped," Amber says.

"She may have hit her head when she fell. It could be a concussion." Terry-Anne is chewing on her lip again. "I'm going to need to make sure she stays awake tonight. I have to keep an eye on her till we can get back to camp in the morning."

"What can we do to help?" I ask.

"I'll manage," Terry-Anne says.

"What if you get too tired and you fall asleep?" Amber asks.

"You have a point," Terry-Anne tells her. "Maybe you girls can do shifts with me. I don't want any of you to be too tired to paddle tomorrow."

Chapter Ten

Which is how we end up pulling our second all-nighter. Although, officially, it may not count as an all-nighter since Terry-Anne only lets each of us stay up for three hours at a time.

I'm on the first shift. When I look at how pale Joon is, and how her hands won't stop shaking, I just want to distract her. My storytelling urge comes back.

What better way is there to keep Joon awake?

Terry-Anne puts a pot of coffee on the fire.

I'm a little surprised when Terry-Anne wants to hear stories about the royal court. "I know they're make-believe," she says as she pokes a marshmallow onto the end of a long twig, "but that doesn't mean they can't be good stories."

"Do you want to hear about the royal greenhouse?" I ask Joon and Terry-Anne. "It's full of exotic flowers, like Bougainvillea, and butterflies. Monarchs, of course." Even Joon, whose head is hurting, laughs when I say that.

"One day," I continue, "a giant frog—the biggest frog I ever saw—he was the size of a car—"

"Was he really that big?" Terry-Anne asks, playing along.

"Bigger," I say. "He was the size of a car and a half. Well, that giant frog broke into the royal greenhouse. He shattered a giant glass window, and the monarchs escaped. Frogs eat butterflies, so you can't blame those butterflies for wanting out. What the monarchs didn't know was that it was winter. They'd lived all their lives in the greenhouse, so they didn't know a thing about winter. Poor creatures were so cold, every part of them shivered. Even their antennae."

"Let me guess what happened next," Terry-Anne says. "Princess Angelica saved the butterflies."

"Don't spoil Jelly's story." Joon sounds a little stronger.

"Princess Angelica didn't have a butterfly net handy," I say, picking up where I left off. "So she used a wire coat hanger."

"How did she make a butterfly net from a coat hanger?" Terry-Anne asks.

"She bent the wire coat hanger to make a round frame. Did I mention the fancy draperies at the royal court?"

"You told us the curtains in Princess Angelica's room were purple velvet," Joon says.

"That's right. But the curtains in the living room were made of the softest gauze. Perfect for a butterfly net. Well, Princess Angelica asked her lady- and gentleman-in-waiting to cut a little fabric off the living room curtains. Just from the bottom, so no one would notice.

Then she caught every single butterfly and returned them all to the greenhouse."

"But what about the giant frog—the one who was the size of one and a half cars? And what about the shattered window? Couldn't the butterflies have flown back out?" Joon asks.

I decide it's a good sign she is paying such close attention to my story.

"Frogs eat butterflies, so the frog took off into the winter weather, following the butterflies as they escaped. And Princess Angelica made a new window. She used the gauzy fabric curtains in place of the glass. A temporary solution, of course, but it worked until the new window arrived. The king and queen put in a rush order."

It's after midnight, and I can feel my head starting to slump over. Terry-Anne says my shift is over and it's time for me to get some rest.

When I wake up, the sun has just begun to rise—and Joon and Terry-Anne are still awake. Amber is finishing her shift.

There is still no cell-phone service, and Terry-Anne wants us to start paddling right after breakfast.

Joon is too weak to do much paddling, but the rudder on the yellow kayak holds, and Amber and Jenna are able to paddle it quickly back to camp in spite of the wind. We make it back in time for lunch.

When the camp director learns what has happened, she gets the camp doctor, who examines Joon.

"I think she may have a mild concussion," the doctor tells us. "It was a good decision to keep Joon up all night. She'll need lots of rest now as she recovers. But I can assure you, she is going to be fine. Even so, I've contacted her parents. They're on their way now to pick her up."

We all cheer when we hear that Joon will be all right. But we're also sad about her leaving camp early.

The doctor raises one finger in the air. He has something more to say. "Is one of you really a princess?" he asks.

I nearly say it's me, but I don't want to get accused of telling lies.

The doctor peers at us through his glasses. "I know Joon is overtired, but during the examination she kept mentioning a friend who was a princess. Something about giant frogs and butterfly nets made of gauze curtains. I must say, it was a fascinating story."

Amber points at me. "Joon must have been talking about Jelly," she tells the doctor. "Aka Princess Angelica."

Chapter Eleven

I hate to give back my purple feather pen, but I know it's the right thing to do. So I bring it to the infirmary, where Joon's parents have come to collect her. The curtains are closed because the doctor wants Joon to rest in a dark room before she and her parents set out for home.

"I'm not really a princess," I tell Joon's parents, holding out the purple pen they sent me.

"You're not?" Joon's father says. "What about that letter you sent us, with the royal seal?"

"It was a pretend seal," I say, hanging my head. "I'm sorry that I lied. I should not have misled you. It's just that..." I stop myself. I am remembering what my dad told me about apologizing. *It's just that* is another way of saying *but*.

Joon is lying on a cot with a cool washcloth on her forehead. When she speaks, she tries not to move so the washcloth won't fall off. "Jelly is good at making up stories," she says. "She's also good at repairing things.

"Terry-Anne told us," Joon's mother says. Then she turns to face me. "We're very grateful that the stories you made up helped keep Joon awake last night, and that you were able to repair the rudder on the kayak."

Joon's father nods in agreement and exchanges a look with his wife. "Because you have been so good to our daughter, we would like you to keep the pen. Even if you're not really royalty."

"Thank you very much," I say, shaking their hands.

The other girls have come to see Joon off. Amber offers to braid Joon's hair before she goes back to the city. Jenna gives Joon her copy of *Scariest Stories*. Maddie makes a list with all our email addresses so that we can stay in touch.

Before she leaves, Joon's mom looks at me. "Why do you think you do it?" she asks.

"Do what?"

"Make up stories."

It's a good question. Only I'm not sure I know the answer. "Pretending to be a princess was fun. It was as if I got to be a different sort of me."

Joon's mother gives me a long look. I can tell she is thinking about what I just said. "It isn't right to lie to others. But as for inventing stories, don't ever stop."

"Thank you," I say to Joon's mother as she steps into the car. I wave my feather pen in the air as they head down the camp driveway.

There is still another week to go before the bus takes us home. How many stories will I make up before then?

Monique Polak is the author of twenty-one books for young people. Long ago, when she went to sleepaway camp, Monique told her bunkmates she was a princess—and they believed her. For more information, visit www.moniquepolak.com.